Prayers, Praises, and Thanksgivings

Prayers, Praises, and Thanksgivings

COMPILED BY
SANDOL STODDARD

PICTURES BY
RACHEL ISADORA

Dial Books · *New York*

To Cynthia Ann Marks Salley
S. S.

For my Aunt Sara and Uncle Mike
R. I.

Published by Dial Books
A Division of Penguin Books USA Inc.
375 Hudson Street
New York, New York 10014

Designed by Sara Reynolds
Printed in the U.S.A.
The full-color artwork was prepared using pencil, black ink,
and watercolor. It was then color-separated and reproduced
as red, blue, yellow, and black halftones.

Contents

PERSONAL ACKNOWLEDGMENTS

This book has been many years in the making. I am grateful for the help and support of many friends who have had a part in it, including especially my editors, Janet Chenery of Dial Books for Young Readers and Barbara Greenman of the Literary Guild; and my agent, Robin Straus. Thanks also to Sara Reynolds and Amelia Lau Carling, the two art directors who designed the book. Mr. Douglas Grant of the Scottish Academic Press in Edinburgh was most kind in obtaining for me a copy of *Hebridean Altars*, by Alistair MacLean, now long out of print, from which I have retrieved several favorite selections. I am also grateful to Mr. Grant and the S.A. Press for permission to reprint quite a number of selections from that splendid treasure-trove of Celtic oral history, *Carmina Gadelica*, by Alexander Carmichael. Meantime, Tom and Coco Mullins have kindly sent me a number of British "graces," while from North Dakota came a Native American prayer courtesy of Bishop George Masuda, and from Rev. Iain Wilson in Wyoming, a stunning Arab Prayer attributed to the woman poet Rabi'ah Al-'Adawiyah, 8th Century. For similar—and other—contributions of many kinds I am greatly indebted to Alice Babin, Gwen Brennick, John Engelcke, Joan Erikson, Terry and Elaine Henry, Jerry Isaak-Shapiro, Lisa Lamers, Madeleine L'Engle, Georgia Mandakis, Jim and Sonya Norton, Lindley Powers, Martha Reeves, Francis B. Sayre, and as always, my family—especially P. R. G.

A NOTE TO READERS

"In religion there are no national boundaries. . . . Lest we forget
the human values that unite us all . . . I pray for a more friendly,
more caring, more understanding human family on this planet."

His Holiness Tenzin Gyatso
The fourteenth Dalai Lama
Winner of the 1989 Nobel Peace Prize

This is a book of many faiths, and many tribes and nations. The voices here are young and old, classic and contemporary, renowned and relatively unknown.

How different we are from one another! Yet our conversations with God bear witness to the fact that we are all members of a single human family.

A child once asked, "If there wasn't a God, who would we thank?" The awakening mind shows a universal need to rejoice in the wonder of Creation. From this follows the desire—in some, a lifelong yearning—to know and understand the Creator.

The world's major religions agree that the path to understanding is also the path of compassion, undertaken even by the smallest child who learns tenderness and respect for others. True prayer comes unbidden from the heart, but its aim is always toward higher standards of behavior.

An individual's *Beginnings* may be repeated many times over, since human growth does not take place as a rocket rises, but as a flower unfolds—or, as a shell spirals. *Reaching Out*, paradoxically, requires greater self-awareness. It is a complex world that we live in, and only as we ourselves become more fully developed do we grasp a sense of its underlying moral order.

The Great Journey of maturity is a theme with infinite variations. Pain and suffering are realities for us all; yet in the name of love, we reach for greater truths. Love itself is the ground of all our being: a wilderness of beauty that we must explore with courage if the human family is to find, and claim at last, its true home in the universe.

Sandol Stoddard

I

Hello God

BEGINNINGS

Lord, teach us to pray.

Saint Luke

God is. I know that.
God made me—I'm glad he did.
God loves me—I need to know that.
I believe in God.

A Child's Prayer
New Zealand

My fingers like to say hello
to each other
whenever I fold my hands,
and I like to say hello
to you, God.
I'm glad I can talk with you
whenever I want.
Thank you for listening.

Lois Walfrid Johnson
U.S.A.

This morning, God
This is your day.
I am your child.
Show me your way.
Amen.

Iona Community
Scotland

You wake me up, Father,
to a new day.
Thanks to you
I'm living.

Help me to live today
as you wish.

A Child's Prayer
Sweden

I am small,
My heart is clean;
Let no one dwell in it
Except God alone.

A Child's Prayer
Germany

Morning has broken
Like the first morning,
Blackbird has spoken
Like the first bird.
Praise for the singing!
Praise for the morning!
Praise for them, springing
Fresh from the Word!

Sweet the rain's new fall
Sunlit from heaven,
Like the first dewfall
On the first grass.
Praise for the sweetness
Of the wet garden,
Sprung in completeness
Where his feet pass.

Mine is the sunlight!
Mine is the morning.
Born of the one light
Eden saw play!
Praise with elation,
Praise every morning,
God's re-creation
Of the new day!

Eleanor Farjeon
England 1881–1965

It is God, the Creator, the Gracious One.
Good morning to you, God, good morning.
I am learning, let me succeed.

A Religious Drum Poem
Ghana

From my head to my feet
I am the image of God.
From my heart to my hands
I feel the breath of God.
When I speak with my mouth
I follow God's will.
When I behold God
Everywhere, in mother, father,
In all dear people,
In beast and flower,
In tree and stone,
Nothing brings fear,
But love to all
That is around me.

Rudolf Steiner
Switzerland 1861–1925

God is light:
And in Him is no darkness at all. . . .

God is not far from every one of us:
In Him we live and move and have our being.

School Prayer-book
England

Dear God,
I belong to you.
Please keep me safe today.
Please help me to be brave,
Help me to tell the truth,
Help me to play fair.

Help me to love my family
And my friends as you love them.

And because you love me,
And all children especially,
Help all the children in the world
Who have no one kind and good
To take care of them today.
Amen.

Irene Wells
U.S.A.

O Lord,
the meal is steaming before us
and it smells good.
The water is clear and fresh.
We are happy and satisfied.
But now we must think of our sisters and brothers
all over the world
who have nothing to eat
and only little to drink.
Please, please give all of them your food
and your drink.
That is most important.
But give them also
what they need every day
to go through this life.
As you gave food and drink
to the people of Israel in the desert
please give it also
to our hungry and thirsty brothers
now and in all times.
Amen.

Prayer of a Young Man
Africa

God bless us, every one!

Charles Dickens
England 1812–1870

Each time we eat,
may we
remember God's love.
Amen.

A Child's Prayer
China

God is great
God is good
And we thank Him
For our food.

Traditional

We thank thee, Lord, for happy hearts,
For rain and sunny weather;
We thank thee, Lord, for this our food,
And that we are together.

Traditional

Scones and pancakes roun' the table,
Eat as much as ye are able,
Eat a'! Pooch nane!*
Hallelujah!
Amen.

Traditional
Scotland

Pooch nane!: Leave nothing!

O you who feed the little bird,
bless our food, O Lord.

Traditional
Norway

For every cup and plateful
God make us truly grateful!

Traditional

Dear Father, hear and bless
Thy beasts and singing birds;
And guard with tenderness
Small things that have no words.

Source Unknown

The year's at the spring
And day's at the morn;
Morning's at seven;
The hillside's dew-pearl'd;
The lark's on the wing;
The snail's on the thorn;
God's in His heaven—
All's right with the world!

Robert Browning
England 1812–1889

The snail does the Holy
Will of God slowly.

Attributed to G. K. Chesterton
England 1874–1936

THE PRAYER OF THE LITTLE DUCKS

Dear God,
give us a flood of water.
Let it rain tomorrow and always.
Give us plenty of little slugs
and other luscious things to eat.
Protect all folk who quack
and everyone who knows how to swim.
Amen.

Carmen De Gasztold
France

Thank God for rain
and the beautiful rainbow colors
and thank God for letting children
splash in the puddles.

A Child's Prayer
England

He prayeth best, who loveth best
All things both great and small;
For the dear God who loveth us,
He made and loveth all.

Samuel Taylor Coleridge
England 1772–1834

O heavenly Father, protect and bless
all things that have breath; guard them from
all evil, and let them sleep in peace.

Albert Schweitzer
Germany/West Africa 1875–1965

Hurt no living thing:
    Ladybird, nor butterfly,
Nor moth with dusty wing,
    Nor cricket chirping cheerily,
Nor grasshopper so light of leap,
    Nor dancing gnat, nor beetle fat,
Nor harmless worms that creep.

Christina Rossetti
England 1830–1894

Little lamb, who made thee?
    Dost thou know who made thee?
Gave thee life and bade thee feed
By the stream and o'er the mead;
Gave thee clothing of delight,
Softest clothing, woolly, bright;
Gave thee such a tender voice,
Making all the vales rejoice?
    Little lamb, who made thee?
    Dost thou know who made thee?

    Little lamb, I'll tell thee;
    Little lamb, I'll tell thee;
He is called by thy name,
For he calls himself a lamb.
He is meek and he is mild,
He became a little child—
I a child and thou a lamb,
We are called by his name.
    Little lamb, God bless thee!
    Little lamb, God bless thee!

William Blake
England 1757–1827

Prayers, Praises, and Thanksgivings

On the shores of Lake Kinneret
There is a most glorious palace,
A garden of God is planted there,
In which no tree moves.

A boy dwells there, like a bird
In the silence of the forest.
There he learns the Torah
From the mouth of Eliyahu.

Hush! Not a wave spouts.
Every bird that flies
Stands and listens,
Absorbing God's Torah.

Yaakov Fichman
Israel

God grows weary of great kingdoms,
but never of little flowers.

Rabindranath Tagore
India 1861–1941

FIREFLY

A little light is going by,
Is going up to see the sky,
A little light with wings.

I never could have thought of it,
To have a little bug all lit
And made to go on wings.

Elizabeth Madox Roberts
U.S.A.

Flowers every night
Blossom in the sky;
Peace in the Infinite;
At peace am I.

Jalal-Ud-Din Rumi
Persia 1207–1273

I see the moon
And the moon sees me.
God bless the moon,
And God bless me.

Source Unknown

All things bright and beautiful,
All creatures great and small,
All things wise and wonderful,
The Lord God made them all.

Each little flower that opens,
Each little bird that sings,
He made their glowing colors,
He made their tiny wings:

The purple-headed mountain,
The river running by,
The sunset and the morning,
That brightens up the sky,

The cold wind in the winter,
The pleasant summer sun,
The ripe fruits in the garden,
He made them every one.

Cecil Frances Alexander
England 1818–1895

Flower in the crannied wall,
I pluck you out of the crannies,
I hold you here, root and all, in my hand,
Little flower—but *if* I could understand
What you are, root and all, and all in all,
I should know what God and man is.

Alfred, Lord Tennyson
England 1809–1892

"Elder Father, though thine eyes
Shine with hoary mysteries,
Canst thou tell what in the heart
Of a cowslip blossom lies?"

"Smaller than all lives that be,
Secret as the deepest sea,
Stands a little house of seeds,
Like an elfin's granary."

"Speller of the stones and weeds,
Skilled in Nature's crafts and creeds,
Tell me what is in the heart
Of the smallest of the seeds."

"God Almighty, and with Him
Cherubim and Seraphim,
Filling all eternity—
Adonai Elohim!"

G. K. Chesterton
England 1874–1936

To see a World in a Grain of Sand
And Heaven in a Wild Flower
Hold Infinity in the palm of your hand
And Eternity in an hour...

William Blake
England 1757–1827

Oh, the Lord is good to me,
And so I thank the Lord,
For giving me the things I need:
The sun, the rain and the appleseed:
The Lord is good to me.

Attributed to Johnny Appleseed
(John Chapman)
U.S.A. 1774–1845

O our Mother the Earth, O our Father the Sky,
Your children are we, and with tired backs
We bring you the gifts that you love.
Then weave for us a garment of brightness;
May the warp be the white light of morning,
May the weft be the red light of evening,
May the fringes be the falling rain,
May the border be the standing rainbow.
Thus weave for us a garment of brightness
That we may walk fittingly where birds sing,
That we may walk fittingly where grass is green,
O our Mother the Earth, O our Father the Sky!

Tewa Indian
North America

What are you, God?
I think I know:
You are the Power
That gives me life
And helps me grow.

Where are you, God?
I think I see
You sometimes in the eyes
And faces of those
Who love me.

But why did you, God,
Make the world so big
And me so small?
That I cannot tell,
At all, at all.

Irene Wells
U.S.A.

Teach me, my God and King,
In all things Thee to see;
And what I do in anything,
To do it as for Thee.

George Herbert
England 1593—1633

'Tis the gift to be simple,
'Tis the gift to be free,
'Tis the gift to come down
Where we ought to be.
And when we find ourselves
In the place just right,
'Twill be in the valley
Of love and delight.
When true simplicity is gain'd,
To bow and to bend
We shan't be asham'd.
To turn, turn will be our delight
'Till by turning, turning,
We come out right.

Traditional: Shaker
U.S.A.

Teach me, Father, how to be
Kind and patient as a tree.
Joyfully the crickets croon
Under shady oak at noon;
Beetle, on his mission bent,
Tarries in that cooling tent.
Let me, also, cheer a spot,
Hidden field or garden grot—
Place where passing souls can rest
  On the way and be their best.

Edwin Markham
U.S.A. 1852–1940

Who has seen the wind?
Neither I nor you:
But when the leaves hang trembling
The wind is passing thro'.

Who has seen the wind?
Neither you nor I:
But when the trees bow down their heads
The wind is passing by.

Christina Rossetti
England 1830–1894

Creator! you who dwell at the ends of the earth
unrivaled, you who gave being and power to men,
saying: let this be man, and to women, saying:
let this be woman! So saying, you made them, shaped them,
gave them being. These you created; watch over them!
Let them be safe and well, unharmed, living in peace.
Where are you? Up in the sky? Or down below?
In clouds? In storms? Hear me, answer me, acknowledge me,
give us perpetual life, hold us forever within your hand.
Receive this offering wherever you are. Creator!

Inca
Peru

Prayers, Praises, and Thanksgivings

Unless you lead me, Lord, I cannot dance.
Would you have me leap and spring,
You yourself, dear Lord, must sing.
So shall I spring with your love,
From your love to understanding,
From understanding to delight.

Mechtild of Magdeburg
Germany 1212–1282

Kum ba yah, my Lord,
Kum ba yah!
Kum ba yah, my Lord,
Kum ba yah!
Kum ba yah, my Lord,
Kum ba yah!

Someone's crying, Lord, Kum ba yah!
Someone's singing, Lord, Kum ba yah!
Someone's praying, Lord, Kum ba yah!

Traditional: Spiritual
Africa

Oh, when the saints
Oh, when the saints
Oh, when the saints go marching in,
Lord I want to be of that number
When the saints go marching in.

Oh, when the sun
Oh, when the sun
Oh, when the sun begins to shine
Lord I want to be of that number
When the sun begins to shine.

Oh, when the band
Oh, when the band
Oh, when the band begins to play
Lord I want to be in that number
When the band begins to play.

Oh, when we all
Oh, when we all
Oh, when we all share bread and wine,
Lord I want to be in that number
When we all share bread and wine.

Oh, when we all
Oh, when we all
Oh, when we all know we belong,
Lord I want to be in that number
When we all know we belong.

Traditional: Spiritual
African American

Let the heavens rejoice, and let the earth be glad;
let the sea thunder and all that is in it;
    let the field be joyful and all that is therein.

Then shall all the trees of the wood shout for joy
before the Lord when he comes,
    when he comes to judge the earth.

He will judge the world with righteousness
    and the peoples with his truth.

Psalm 96

Are you ready when the Lord shall come?
Are you ready when the Lord shall come?
In the morning five o'clock,
In the morning six o'clock.
Are you ready when the Lord shall come?

Traditional: Spiritual
West Africa

Glory to Thee, glory to Thee, O Lord,
O Lord of the Universe, O Sovereign God:
Glory to Thee, O Creator. Glory to
Thee, O Holy God.

Dadu
India 1544–1603

Joshua fit the battle of Jericho, Jericho,
   Jericho,
Joshua fit the battle of Jericho,
And the walls came tumbling down.

You may talk about your king of Gideon,
You may talk about your man of Saul,
But there's none like good old Joshua
At the battle of Jericho.

Up to the walls of Jericho
He marched with spear in hand.
"Go blow them ram-horns," Joshua cried,
" 'Cause the battle am in my hand."

Then the ram-horns began to blow,
Trumpets began to sound.
Joshua commanded the children to shout,
And the walls came tumbling down, that morning,
The walls came tumbling down.

Joshua fit the battle of Jericho, Jericho,
    Jericho,
Joshua fit the battle of Jericho,
And the walls came tumbling down.

Traditional: Spiritual
African American

Our Father in heaven,
Hallowed be your Name,
Your Kingdom come,
Your will be done,
On earth as in heaven.
Give us today our daily bread.
Forgive us our sins
As we forgive those
Who sin against us.
Save us from the time of trial,
And deliver us from evil.
For the kingdom, the power,
And the glory are yours,
Now and forever.
Amen.

Book of Common Prayer

God before me, God behind me,
God above me, God below me;
I on the path of God,
God upon my track.

Who is there on land?
Who is there on wave?
Who is there on billow?
Who is there by door-post?
Who is along with us?
God and Lord.

Ancient Celtic Prayer
The Hebrides

Protect me, O Lord;
My boat is so small,
And your sea is so big.

Ancient Breton Prayer
France

When bad things happen to me, God,
You see and you care—
I know that—
                    No matter what.

When I am hurt and afraid
You will be there—
I know that—
                    No matter what.

Bigger than any pain,
Stronger than any fear,
You have the power to love me,
And help me, and save me—
                    No matter what.

Irene Wells
U.S.A.

O God, make speed to save us,
O Lord, make haste to help us....

Book of Common Prayer

Hello God   33

Oh, the Lord looked down from his window in the sky,
Said: "I created man, but I can't remember why!
Nothing but fighting since creation day.
I'll send a little water and wash them all away."
Oh, the Lord came down and looked around a spell.
There was Mr. Noah behaving mighty well.
And that is the reason the Scriptures record
Noah found grace in the eyes of the Lord.

    Noah found grace in the eyes of the Lord,
    Noah found grace in the eyes of the Lord,
    Noah found grace in the eyes of the Lord,
    And He left him high and dry.

The Lord said: "Noah, there's going to be a flood,
There's going to be some water, there's going to be some mud,
So take off your hat, Noah, take off your coat,
Get Shem, Ham, and Japeth and build yourself a boat."
Noah said: "Lord, I don't believe I could."
The Lord said: "Noah, get yourself some wood.
You never know what you can do till you try.
Build it fifty cubits wide and thirty cubits high."

    Noah found grace in the eyes of the Lord. . . .

Noah said: "There she is, there she is, Lord!"
The Lord said: "Noah, it's time to get aboard.
Take of each creature a he and a she,
And of course take Mrs. Noah and the whole family."
Noah said: "Lord, it's getting mighty dark."
The Lord said: "Noah, get those creatures in the ark."
Noah said: "Lord, it's beginning to pour."
The Lord said: "Noah, hurry up and close the door."
    Noah found grace in the eyes of the Lord. . . .

The ark rose up on the bosom of the deep.
After forty days Mr. Noah took a peep.
He said: "We're not moving, Lord, where are we at?"
The Lord said: "You're sitting right on Mount Ararat."
Noah said: "Lord, it's getting nice and dry."
The Lord said: "Noah, see my rainbow in the sky.
Take all your creatures and people the earth,
And be sure that you're not more trouble than you're worth."
    Noah found grace in the eyes of the Lord. . . .

Traditional: Spiritual
African American

Our Father in heaven:
Please forgive me for the wrongs I have done:
For bad temper and angry words;
For being greedy and wanting the best for myself;
For making other people unhappy:
Forgive me, heavenly Father.

Dick Williams
England

O God, you have let us pass the day in peace,
Let us pass the night in peace,
O Lord, you have no Lord,
There is no strength but in you.
There is no unity but in your house.
Under your hand we pass the night.
You are our mother and our father.
You are our home.
Amen.

Iona Community
Scotland

In my little bed I lie,
God, my Father, hear my cry;
Please protect me through the night,
Keep me safe till morning light.
Amen.

A Child's Prayer
Pakistan

From warlocks, witches and wurricoes,
From ghosties, ghoulies and long-legged beasties
From all things that go "bump" in the night
Good Lord deliver us.

Ancient Cornish Litany
England

Be Thy right hand, O God, under my head,
Be Thy light, O Spirit, over me shining.
And be the cross of the nine angels over me down
From the crown of my head to the soles of my feet,
From the crown of my head to the soles of my feet.

Ancient Celtic Prayer
The Hebrides

Keep us, O Lord, as the apple of your eye;
Hide us under the shadow of your wings.

Book of Common Prayer

Father, bless me in my body,
Father, bless me in my soul.
Father, bless me this night
In my body and my soul.

Ancient Celtic Prayer
The Hebrides

Silent night,
Holy night,
All is calm,
All is bright
Round yon virgin
Mother and child.
Holy infant so tender and mild,
Sleep in heavenly peace,
Sleep in heavenly peace.

Traditional Carol
Germany

What child is this,
Who, laid to rest,
On Mary's lap is sleeping?
Whom angels greet
With anthems sweet,
While shepherds watch are keeping?

This, this is Christ the King,
Whom shepherds guard
And angels sing:
Haste, haste to bring him laud,*
The babe, the son of Mary.

Traditional Carol
England

*laud: praise

Hush! my dear, lie still and slumber,
Holy angels guard thy bed;
Heavenly blessings, without number,
Gently falling on thy head.

Isaac Watts
England 1674–1748

What can I give him,
Poor as I am?
If I were a shepherd,
I would bring a lamb,
If I were a wise man,
I would do my part;
Yet what can I give him—
Give him my heart.

Christina Rossetti
England 1830–1894

Jesus Christ, Thou child so wise,
Bless mine hands and fill mine eyes,
And bring my soul to Paradise.

Hilaire Belloc
England 1870–1953

God bless all those that I love;
God bless all those that love me;
God bless all those that love those that I love;
And all those that love those that love me.

Old New England Sampler

O God of light, God of might
Keep me ever in thy sight
Grant my eyes to safely sleep
While you dear Lord my soul shall keep.

David Adam
England

The Lord bless us, and keep us:
the Lord make his face to shine upon us,
and be gracious to us.
The Lord lift up his countenance upon us,
and give us peace.

Book of Common Prayer

II

Wings of Freedom

REACHING OUT

I, _____
am here, Lord.

I don't need to be alone at the top of a tree
to talk to you.

Just help me
to be quiet within myself,
so that, like Elijah,
I can listen for you.

Although you do not come
in a great noise,
I can hear you
and you can hear me.

Spirit of God, in me,
help me to pray
in the way best for me.

Joan M. Burns
England

Each day the first day:
Each day a life.

Dag Hammarskjöld
Sweden 1905–1961

O God, Creator of Light: at the rising
of your sun this morning, let the greatest
of all light, your love,
rise like the sun within our hearts.
Amen.

Armenian Apostolic Church
Lebanon

Eternal God
We say good morning to you.
Hallowed be your name.
Early in the morning, before we begin our work
We praise your glory.
Renew our bodies as fresh as the morning flowers.
Open our inner eyes, as the sun casts new light
    upon the darkness which prevailed over the night.
Deliver us from all captivity.
Give us wings of freedom, like the birds in the sky,
To begin a new journey. . . .

Masao Takenaka
Japan

You are to me, O Lord,
What wings are to the flying bird.

Source Unknown
Hindu

Thou dawnest beautifully in the horizon
    of the sky,
O living Aton who wast the Beginning of life!
When thou didst rise in the eastern horizon,
Thou didst fill every land with thy beauty.
Thou art beautiful, great, glittering, high over
    every land,
Thy rays, they encompass the lands, even to the end
    of all that thou hast made. . . .
How manifold are thy works!
They are hidden before men,
O sole God, beside whom there is no other.
Thou didst create the earth according to thy heart.

Ancient Egyptian Hymn

Open thou our lips, O Lord, and purify
our hearts, that we may offer thee a
service worthy of thy holy name.

Christina Rossetti
England 1830–1894

God is love and we are his children.
There is no room for fear in love.
We love because he loved us first.

Scottish Liturgy

Not because we know how to pray,
but because we know our need of you.
Look kindly, Lord, on what we ask
and answer us when the time is right.
Amen.

Iona Community
Scotland

Not my brother, not my sister
but it's me, O Lord,
Standing in the need of prayer,
Standing in the need of prayer.

Not my mother, not my father
but it's me, O Lord,
Standing in the need of prayer,
Standing in the need of prayer.

Not my neighbor, not a stranger
but it's me, O Lord,
Standing in the need of prayer.
Standing in the need of prayer.

Traditional: Spiritual
African American

O Lord, Thou knowest how
busy I must be this day.
If I forget Thee,
do not forget me.

Jacob Astley
England 1579–1652

Back of the loaf is the snowy flour,
And back of the flour the mill;
And back of the mill is the wheat, and the shower,
And the sun, and the Father's will.

M. D. Babcock
England 1858–1901

May all who share
These gifts today
Be blessed by Thee,
We humbly pray.

What God gives
And what we take
'Tis a gift
For Christ his sake;

Be the meal
Of beans or peas,
God be thanked
For those and these;

Have we flesh
Or have we fish,
All are fragments
From His dish.

Robert Herrick
England 1591–1674

Give us grateful hearts, our Father,
for all your mercies, and make us
mindful of the needs of others.
Amen.

Book of Common Prayer

Us and this,
God bless.

Old Quaker Grace

O God, make us able
For all that's on the table!
Amen.

*Traditional
Ireland*

To Life!

Traditional Jewish Toast

Baby's heart is lifted up
For eggs laid into the cup.
Yellow stained her praising lips
With the bread and butter strips.

Aged cripples by the bed
Frugal feast on milk and bread,
And the swarthy brigand men
Eat risotto in their den.

Praise God who giveth meat
Convenient unto all to eat:
Praise for tea and buttered toast,
Father, Son and Holy Ghost.

R. L. Gales
England

For water-ices, cheap but good,
That find us in a thirsty mood;
For ices made of milk or cream
That slip down smoothly as a dream;
For cornets, sandwiches and pies
That make the gastric juices rise;
For ices bought in little shops
Or at the kerb from him who stops;
For chanting of the sweet refrain:
"Vanilla, strawberry or plain?"
We thank Thee, Lord, who sendst with heat
This cool deliciousness to eat.

Allan M. Laing
England

Give to us eyes
That we may truly see,
Flight of a bird,
The shapes in a tree,
Curve of a hillside,
Colours in a stone,
Give to us seeing eyes,
O Lord, our God.

Give to us ears
That we may truly hear,
Music in birdsong,
Rippling water clear,
Whine of the winter wind,
Laughter of a friend,
Give to us hearing ears,
O Lord, our God.

Give to us hands
That we may truly know,
Patterns in tree bark,
Crispness of the snow,
Smooth feel of velvet,
Shapes in a shell,
Give to us knowing hands,
O Lord, our God.

Iona Community
Scotland

Our father, hear us, and our grandfather. I mention also
all those that shine, the yellow day, the good wind,
the good timber, and the good earth.
All the animals, listen to me under the ground. Animals
above ground, and water animals, listen to me. We shall
eat your remnants of food. Let them be good.
Let there be long breath and life. Let the people increase,
the children of all ages, the girls and the boys, and the
men of all ages and the women, the old men of all ages
and the old women. The food will give us strength
whenever the sun runs.
Listen to us, Father, Grandfather. We ask thought, heart,
love, happiness. We are going to eat.

Arapaho Indian
North America

O Lord, grant us to love Thee; grant that we may love
those that love Thee; grant that we may do
the deeds that win Thy love.
Make the love of Thee be dearer to us than ourselves,
than our families, than wealth, and even
than cool water.

Mohammed
Arabia 570–632

Lord, help me to find the good and praise it.

Source Unknown

For I will consider my cat Jeoffrey.

For he is the servant of the Living God, duly and daily
serving him.

For at the first glance of the glory of God in the East he
worships in his way.

For this is done by wreathing his body seven times around
with elegant quickness.

For then he leaps up to catch the musk, which is the blessing
of God upon his prayer.

For he rolls upon prank to work it in.

For having done duty and received blessing he begins to consider
himself.

For this he performs in ten degrees.

For first he looks upon his fore-paws to see if they are clean.

For secondly he kicks up behind to clear away there.

For thirdly he works it upon stretch with the fore-paws extended.

For fourthly he sharpens his paws by wood.

For fifthly he washes himself.

For sixthly he rolls upon wash.

For seventhly he fleas himself, that he may not be interrupted
upon the beat.

For eighthly he rubs himself against a post.

For ninthly he looks up for his instructions.

For tenthly he goes in quest of food.

For having considered God and himself he will consider his neighbor.

For if he meets another cat he will kiss her in kindness.

For when he takes his prey he plays with it to give it a chance.

For one mouse in seven escapes by his dallying.

For when his day's work is done his business more properly begins.

For he keeps the Lord's watch in the night against the adversary.

For he counteracts the powers of darkness by his electrical skin
and glaring eyes.
For he counteracts the Devil, who is death, by brisking about the life.
For in his morning orisons he loves the sun and the sun loves him.
For he is of the tribe of Tiger.

Christopher Smart
England 1722–1771

Tyger Tyger, burning bright,
In the forests of the night:
What immortal hand or eye
Could frame thy fearful symmetry?

In what distant deeps or skies
Burnt the fire of thine eyes?
On what wings dare he aspire?
What the hand, dare seize the fire?

And what shoulders, & what art,
Could twist the sinews of thy heart?
And when thy heart began to beat,
What dread hand? & what dread feet?

What the hammer? what the chain?
In what furnace was thy brain?
What the anvil? what dread grasp,
Dare its deadly terrors clasp?

When the stars threw down their spears
And water'd heaven with their tears:
Did he smile his work to see?
Did he who made the Lamb make thee?

Tyger, Tyger burning bright,
In the forests of the night:
What immortal hand or eye,
Dare frame thy fearful symmetry?

William Blake
England 1757–1827

I am the Turquoise Woman's son
On top of Belted Mountain beautiful horses
Slim like a weasel

My horse has a hoof like striped agate
His fetlock is like fine eagle plume
His legs are like quick lightning

My horse's body is like an eagle-feathered arrow

My horse has a tail like a trailing black cloud

I put flexible goods on my horse's back
The Holy Wind blows through his mane
His mane is made of rainbows

My horse's ears are made of round corn

My horse's eyes are made of stars

My horse's head is made of mixed waters
    (from the holy waters)
    (he never knows thirst)

My horse's teeth are made of white shell

The long rainbow is in his mouth for a bridle
With it I guide him. . . .

Before me peaceful
Behind me peaceful
Under me peaceful
Over me peaceful
Peaceful voice when he neighs
I am everlasting and peaceful
I stand for my horse.

Navaho Indian
North America

Lord, Thou mighty River, all-knowing, all-seeing,
And I like a little fish in thy great waters,
How shall I sound Thy depths?
How shall I reach Thy shores?
Wherever I go, I see Thee only.

> Guru Nanak
> *Pakistan 1469–1539*

Wisdom of serpent be thine
Wisdom of raven be thine,
Wisdom of valiant eagle.

Voice of swan be thine,
Voice of honey be thine,
Voice of the son of the stars.

Bounty of sea be thine,
Bounty of land be thine,
Bounty of the Father of heaven.

> *Ancient Celtic Blessing*
> *The Hebrides*

When I walk through thy woods,
may my right foot and my left foot
be harmless to the little creatures
that move in its grasses: as it is said
by the mouth of thy prophet,
They shall not hurt nor destroy
in all my holy mountain.
Amen.

> Rabbi Moshe Hakotun
> *18th c. (?)*

Praised be my Lord God for all his creatures,
      and especially for our brother the sun, who brings
      us the day and who brings us the light; fair is he
      and shines with a very great splendor. . . .
Praised be my Lord for our sister the moon, and for
      the stars, the which he has set clear and lovely
      in heaven.
Praised be my Lord for our brother the wind, and for
      air and cloud, calms and all weather. . . .
Praised be my Lord for our sister water, who is very
      serviceable unto us and humble and precious and clean.
Praised be my Lord for our brother fire, through whom
      thou givest us light in darkness, and he is bright
      and pleasant and very mighty and strong.
Praised be my Lord for our mother the earth, the which
      doth sustain us and keep us, and bringeth forth divers
      fruits and flowers of many colors, and grass. . . .
Praise ye and bless my Lord, and give Him thanks, and
      serve Him with great humility.

St. Francis of Assisi
Italy 1181–1226

They furnish shade to others
While standing in the sun themselves;
The fruit they bear is for others' sake.
Thus, good men are like trees.

Ancient Sanskrit
India

All is silent.
In the still and soundless air,
I fervently bow
To my Almighty God.

Hsieh Ping-hsin
China

For cities and towns, factories and farms, flowers
     and trees, sea and sky—
Lord, we praise You for the world and its beauty.
For family and friends, neighbors and cousins—
Lord, we thank You for friendship and love.
For kind hearts, smiling faces, and helping hands—
Lord, we praise You for those who care for others.
For commandments that teach us how to live—
Lord, we thank You for those who help us to understand
     your laws.
And for making us one family on earth, the children
     of One God—
Lord, we praise You, who made all people different,
     yet alike.

Jewish Liturgy

A child said, *"What is the grass?"* fetching it
    to me with full hands.
What could I answer the child? I do not know what
    it is any more than he.
. . . I guess it is the handkerchief of the Lord,
A scented gift and remembrance designedly dropped,
Bearing the owner's name some way in the corners,
    that we may see and remark, and say, *"Whose?"*

Walt Whitman
U.S.A. 1819–1892

Sandpipers running along the beach,
The birds overhead crying,
The beauty of a lush green field,
A cow's contented sighing,
The whistle of the wind through trees,
The gurgle of a brook:
All these mean peace to me—
Though not the lack of war—
They mean to me the inner peace,
The peace of solitude.

Joseph A. P. Spencer
U.S.A. 1955–1970

O God, who hast made all things beautiful:
give me a love of Thy countryside, its lanes
and meadows, its woods and streams, and clean
open spaces; and let me keep it fresh and
unspoilt for those who shall come after me.
Amen.

School Prayer-book
England

In Heaven,
Some little blades of grass
Stood before God.
"What did you do?"
Then all save one of the little blades
Began eagerly to relate
The merits of their lives.
This one stayed a small way behind,
Ashamed. Presently God said,
"And what did you do?"
The little blade answered, "Oh, my Lord,
Memory is bitter to me,
For, if I did good deeds,
I know not of them."
Then God, in all his splendor,
Arose from his throne.
"Oh, best little blade of grass!" he said.

Stephen Crane
U.S.A. 1871–1900

Our Pacific islands are yours, O Lord,
And all the seas that surround them.
You made the palm trees grow,
And the birds fly in the air.

When we see your beautiful rising sun
And hear the waves splash on our shores,
When we see the new moon rise
And the old moon sink,

We know, Lord, how wonderful you are.
You bless our people;
From Truk to Tonga and beyond
You spread your caring wings.

Even when we sail through stormy seas,
And fly amidst rain clouds,
We know you await us,
With Kai-kai* and coconut.

You who turn storms into gentle winds,
And troubled seas into tranquil waters,
You who make yams grow
And bananas blossom,

Wash our people with justice;
Teach us with righteousness;
Speak to us daily;
Strengthen us to serve you.

Bernard Narokobi
Papua, New Guinea

Kai-kai: food, feasting

Let my thoughts and words please you, Lord.
Send me round the world in my prayers
with the news of your goodness.

Joan M. Burns
England

Bless to us, O God, the earth beneath our feet
Bless to us the path whereon we go. . . .

Iona Community
Scotland

Give me my scallop shell of quiet,
My staff of faith to walk upon,
My scrip of joy, immortal diet,
My bottle of salvation:
My gown of glory, hope's true gauge,
And thus I'll take my pilgrimage. . . .

Sir Walter Raleigh
England 1552–1618

Alone with none but Thee, my God,
I journey on my way;
What need I fear when Thou art near,
O King of night and day?
More safe am I within Thy hand
Than if a host did round me stand.

Attributed to St. Columba
Ireland/Scotland c. 521–597

Hear me, four quarters of the world—a
relative I am! Give me the strength to walk
the soft earth. . . . Give me the eyes to see
and the strength to understand, that I may be
like you. With your power only can I face
the winds. Great Spirit. . . all over the earth
the faces of living things are all alike.
With tenderness have these come up out of the
ground. Look upon these faces of children
without number and with children in their arms,
that they may face the winds and walk the
good road to the day of quiet. This is my
prayer; hear me!

Black Elk
Sioux Indian
North America

In Tsegihi
In the house made of dawn,
In the house made of evening twilight,
In the house made of dark cloud,
In the house made of rain and mist, of pollen, of grasshoppers,

The path to which is on the rainbow,
Where the zigzag lightning stands high on top,
O male divinity!
With your moccasins of dark cloud, come to us. . . .
With the far darkness made of the rain and the mist. . . .
With the zigzag lightning, with the rainbow hanging high
      on the ends of your wings, come to us, soaring.
With the near darkness made of the dark cloud of the rain
      and mist, come to us,
With the darkness on the earth, come to us.
With these I wish the foam floating on the flowing water
      over the roots of the great corn. . . .
Happily may fair yellow corn, fair blue corn, fair corn
      of all kinds, plants of all kinds, to the ends
      of the earth, come with you. . . .
Thus you accomplish your tasks.
Happily the old men will regard you,
The young men and the young women will regard you,
The children will regard you. . . .
May their roads home be on the trail of peace,
Happily may they all return.
In beauty I walk,
With beauty before me I walk,
With beauty behind me, I walk,
With beauty above and about me, I walk.
It is finished in beauty.
It is finished in beauty.

Navaho Indian
North America

Go well and safely,
Go well and safely,
Go well and safely,
The Lord be ever with you.

Zulu
Africa

This train don't carry no gamblers, this train,
This train don't carry no gamblers, this train,
This train don't carry no gamblers, no hard sports or
    midnight ramblers,
This train don't carry no gamblers, this train.

This train don't carry no loafers, this train,
This train don't carry no loafers, this train,
This train don't carry no loafers, no smart skippers or
    cigarette smokers,
This train don't carry no loafers, this train.

This train is bound for glory, this train,
This train is bound for glory, this train,
This train is bound for glory, there to shout and tell a story.
This train is bound for glory, this train.

Traditional: Spiritual
U.S.A.

I am young
And my tomorrows are plenty,
so my faults
will not hold me down.
For my faith
though it be weak,
makes me strong:
For my tomorrows are plenty.

Robbie Walker
Maori
New Zealand

Good for good is only fair;
Bad for bad soon brings despair;
Bad for good is vile and base;
Good for bad shows forth God's grace.

Welsh Folk Saying

Good Lord, help me to win if I may,
and if I may not, help me to be
a good loser.

Source Unknown

In the name of God,
May he protect us,
May he support us:
May we go forward together,
True comrades:

May our search after truth find its fruit:
May we never hold in our hearts
Ill-will the one for the other:

In the name of God,
Peace.

Schoolboys' Prayer
India

Peace between neighbors,
Peace between kindred,
Peace between lovers,
In love of the King of life.

Peace between person and person,
Peace between wife and husband,
Peace between woman and children,
The peace of Christ above all peace.

Ancient Celtic
The Hebrides

Goodness is stronger than evil,
Love is stronger than hate,
Light is stronger than darkness,
Life is stronger than death.
Victory is ours
Through Him who loved us.

Archbishop Desmond Tutu
South Africa

Fill Your children with kindness,
wisdom, and love. Then shall they learn
to live at peace. Blessed is the Lord,
Teacher of Peace.

Jewish Liturgy

To believe in God
is to know the world is round
not flat,
and there is no edge of anything.

Nowadays
to be on your way
is to be home.

Joseph Pintauro
U.S.A.

Dear Lord, you are the Truth. When I keep
myself rooted in you, I will live in the Truth.
Help me, Lord, to live a truthful life, a life
in which I am guided not by popularity, public
opinion, current fashion or convenient formu-
lations but by a knowledge that comes from knowing
you. . . . Lord, bring me always closer to you who
are my teacher, always teaching me out of love.
Amen.

Henri J. M. Nouwen
U.S.A.

Hoping is knowing that there is love,
it is trust in tomorrow
it is falling asleep
and waking again
when the sun rises.
In the midst of a gale at sea,
it is to discover land.
In the eyes of another
it is to see that he understands you. . . .
As long as there still is hope
There will also be prayer. . . .
And God will be holding you
in his hands.

Source Unknown
Cited by Henri J. M. Nouwen
U.S.A.

Creating God, your fingers trace
The bold designs of farthest space;
Let sun and moon and stars and light
And what lies hidden praise your might.

Sustaining God, your hands uphold
Earth's mysteries known or yet untold;
Let water's fragile blend with air,
Enabling life, proclaim your care.

Redeeming God, your arms embrace
All now despised for creed or race;
Let peace, descending like a dove,
Make known on earth your healing love.

Indwelling God, your gospel claims
One family with a billion names;
Let every life be touched by grace
Until we praise you face to face.

Jeffery Rowthorn
U.S.A.

Where can I go then from your Spirit?
  Where can I flee from your presence?

If I climb up to heaven, you are there;
  if I make the grave my bed, you are there also.

If I take the wings of the morning
  and dwell in the uttermost parts of the sea,

Even there your hand will lead me
  and your right hand hold me fast.

If I say, "Surely the darkness will cover me,
  and the light around me turn to night,"

Darkness is not dark to you;
  the night is as bright as the day;
  darkness and light to you are both alike. . . .

I will thank you because I am marvelously made;
  your works are wonderful, and I know it well.

Psalm 139

O Lord, my day's work is over; bless all
that I have done aright, and forgive all
that has been wrong; and for the remaining
hours of this day grant me the peace and rest
that come from thee alone.

A Franciscan Prayer

Thanks for today, God ... for all of it:
   For the friends I saw ...
   For the beauty around me ...
   For work to do ...
Thanks for today, God ... for all of it:
   For mistakes discovered ...
   For sins forgiven ...
   For angry words unspoken ...
Thanks for today, God ... for all of it, every bit.
Amen.

Helen F. Couch and Sam S. Barefield
U.S.A.

Lord of the springtime, Father of flower,
field and fruit, smile on us in these
earnest days when the work is heavy and
the toil wearisome; lift up our hearts,
O God, to the things worthwhile—
sunshine and night, the dripping rain,
the song of the birds, books and music,
and the voices of our friends. Lift up
our hearts to these this night, O Father,
and grant us Thy peace.
Amen.

W. E. B. Du Bois
U.S.A./Ghana 1868–1963

O thou great Chief, light a candle
within my heart that I may see what is
therein and sweep the rubbish from
thy dwelling-place.

Prayer of an African Girl

Bad I am, but yet thy child.
Father, be thou reconciled.
Spare thou me, since I see
With thy might that thou art mild.

Gerard Manley Hopkins
Wales 1844–1889

Even if I have gone astray, I am
thy child, O God; thou art my father
and mother.

Arjan (Sikh)
India 17th c.

Thou art my father: who is my mother,
who is my father? Only thou, O God.

Kekchi Tribe
Central America

God is Father and Mother:
the Father of fathers,
and the Mother of mothers.

God is the One, the One who has made
all things. God is a Spirit, the Spirit
of spirits... the divine Spirit.

Ancient Egyptian Hymn

In the One you are never alone,
In the One you are always at home.

Dag Hammarskjöld
Sweden 1905–1961

Everyone to his own.
The bird is in the sky,
The stone rests in the land.
In water lives the fish,
My spirit in God's hand.

Angelus Silesius
Poland 1624–1677

I find thee throned in my heart,
    my Lord Jesus.
It is enough.
I know that thou art throned in heaven:
My heart and heaven are one.

Alistair MacLean
Scotland 1922–1987

All praise to Thee, my God, this night
For all the blessing of the light;
Keep me, oh keep me, King of Kings,
Beneath Thine own Almighty wings.

Thomas Ken
England 1637–1711

A NUN'S PRAYER

Lord, let me adore you while I sleep;
Do not let me be separated from you.
Mother Mary, pray for me.
Holy saints and hermits, pray for me,
Holy angels guard me, and send me good
dreams.

Maggie Ross
U.S.A.

QUEEN'S PRAYER

O kou aloha no
Aia i ka lani,
A 'o kou 'oia'i'o
Hemolele ho'i.

Your love
Is in heaven
And your truth
So perfect.

Ko'u noho mihi 'ana
A pa'ahao 'ia
'O 'oe ku'u lama,
Kou nani, ko'u ko'o.

I live in sorrow
Imprisoned,
You are my light,
Your glory my support.

Mai nana 'ino'ino
Na hewa o kanaka,
Aka e huikala
A ma'ema'e no.

Behold not with malevolence
The sins of man,
But forgive
And cleanse.

No laila e ka Haku,
Ma lalo o kou 'eheu
Ko makou maluhina
A mau aku no.

And so, o Lord,
Beneath your wings
Be our peace
Forever more.

Queen Liliuokalani
Hawaii 1838–1917

O give thanks unto the Lord,
for He is good,
For His mercy
endureth for ever.

Psalm 136

The Lord is my shepherd; I shall not want.
He maketh me to lie down in green pastures:
    he leadeth me beside the still waters.
He restoreth my soul: he leadeth me in the paths
    of righteousness for his name's sake.
Yea, though I walk through the valley of the shadow of death,
    I will fear no evil: for thou art with me;
    thy rod and thy staff they comfort me.
Thou preparest a table before me in the presence
    of mine enemies; thou anointest my head with oil;
    my cup runneth over.
Surely goodness and mercy shall follow me
    all the days of my life:
    and I will dwell in the house of the Lord for ever.

Psalm 23

Let nothing disturb you.
Let nothing frighten you.
Everything passes.
God never changes.
Patience wins out over all.
To him who has God
Nothing is lacking.
God alone satisfies.

St. Teresa of Avila
Spain 1515–1582

Keep watch, dear Lord, with those who work,
or watch, or weep this night, and give your
angels charge over those who sleep.
Tend the sick, Lord Christ; give rest to
the weary, bless the dying, soothe the
suffering, pity the afflicted, shield the
joyous; and all for your love's sake. Amen.

St. Augustine
North Africa 354–430

Deep peace of the running wave to you,
Deep peace of the flowing air to you,
Deep peace of the quiet earth to you,
Deep peace of the sleeping stones to you. . . .

Deep peace, deep peace. . .
In the name of the Three who are One,
And by the will of the King of the Elements,
Peace! Peace!

Fiona McLeod
Scotland

III

Lord of the Dance

T H E   G R E A T   J O U R N E Y

Let the words of my mouth and the
meditation of my heart
be acceptable in your sight,
O Lord, my strength and my redeemer.

Psalm 19

I believe that life is given us so we may
grow in love, and I believe that God is in me
as the sun is in the color and fragrance
of a flower—the Light in my darkness,
the Voice in my silence.

Helen Keller
U.S.A. 1880–1968

O high and glorious God,
light up my heart.

St. Francis of Assisi
Italy 1181–1226

Holy, holy, holy Lord, God of power and might,
heaven and earth are full of your glory.
Hosanna in the highest:
Blessed is he who comes in the name of the Lord.
Hosanna in the highest.

Book of Common Prayer

O Lord, help me to greet the coming day in peace.
Help me in all things to rely on thy holy will.
Bless my dealings with all who surround me. . . .
In unforeseen events let me not forget that all
are sent by thee. . . . Direct my will, teach me
to pray, pray thou thyself in me.

Metropolitan Philaret of Moscow
Russia 19th c.

Father, may I so live the life of love
this day that all those with whom I have
anything to do may be as sure of love
in the world as they are of the sunlight.

Source Unknown
U.S.A.

Thou art the sky and thou art the nest as well.
O thou beautiful, there in the nest it is thy love
     that encloses the soul with colours and
     sounds and odours.
There comes the morning with the golden basket in
     her right hand bearing the wreath of beauty,
     silently to crown the earth. . . .

Rabindranath Tagore
India 1861–1941

I arise today
Through the strength of heaven:
Light of sun,
Radiance of moon,
Splendor of fire,
Speed of lightning,
Swiftness of wind,
Depth of sea,
Stability of earth,
Firmness of rock.

I arise today
Through God's strength to pilot me:
God's wisdom to uphold me,
God's eye to look before me,
God's ear to hear me,
God's word to speak for me,
God's hand to guard me,
God's way to lie before me,
God's host to save me. . . .

Attributed to St. Patrick
Ireland 389(?)–461

Bless to me, O God,
Each thing mine eye sees;
Bless to me, O God,
Each sound mine ear hears;
Bless to me, O God,
Each odour that goes to my nostrils;
Bless to me, O God,
Each taste that goes to my lips. . . .

Ancient Celtic Prayer
The Hebrides

Dear Lord my God,
Good morning!

The rain is falling
to wake the wintry world,
to green the grass,
to bring blossoms to the tree
outside my window.

The world and I wake up for you.
Alleluia!

Madeleine L'Engle
U.S.A.

Let us in peace eat the food
that God has provided for us.
Praise be to God for all
his gifts. Amen.

Armenian Apostolic Church
Lebanon

Prayers, Praises, and Thanksgivings

O Lord, that lends me life,
Lend me a heart replete with thankfulness!

William Shakespeare
England 1564–1616

Thou that hast given so much to me,
Give one thing more—a grateful heart:
Not thankful when it pleaseth me,
As if thy blessings had spare days,
But such a heart whose Pulse may be
Thy Praise.

George Herbert
England 1593–1633

There is a mother's heart in the heart
of God. And 'tis his delight to break
the bread of love and truth
for his children.

Alistair MacLean
Scotland 1922–1987

Some hae meat and canna eat
And some wad eat that want it.
But we hae meat and we can eat,
And sae the Lord be thankit.

Robert Burns
Scotland 1759–1796

Give me a good digestion, Lord,
And also something to digest.
Give me a healthy body, Lord,
With sense to keep it at its best.

Give me a healthy mind, Lord,
To keep the good and pure in sight,
Which, seeing sin, is not appalled,
But finds a way to set it right.

Give me a mind that is not bored,
That does not whimper, whine or sigh;
Don't let it worry overmuch
About the fussy thing called I.

Give me a sense of humor, Lord,
Give me the grace to see a joke,
To get some happiness from life
And pass it on to other folk.

Thomas H. B. Webb
England 1898–1917

Heavenly Father, bless us,
And keep us all alive;
There's ten of us to dinner
And not enough for five.

Source Unknown
England 19th c.

It is a comely fashion to be glad;
Joy is the grace we say to God.

> Socrates
> *Greece c. 470 B.C.–399 B.C.*

From silly devotions
and from sour-faced saints,
good Lord, deliver us.

> St. Teresa of Ávila
> *Spain 1515–1582*

i thank You God for most this amazing
day: for the leaping greenly spirits of trees
and a blue true dream of sky; and for everything
which is natural which is infinite which is yes

(i who have died am alive again today,
and this is the sun's birthday; this is the birth
day of life and of love and wings: and of the gay
great happening illimitably earth)

how should tasting touching hearing seeing
breathing any—lifted from the no
of all nothing—human merely being
doubt unimaginable You?

(now the ears of my ears awake and
now the eyes of my eyes are opened)

> e. e. cummings
> *U.S.A. 1894–1962*

O Lord my God, how excellent is your greatness!
you are clothed with majesty and splendor.

You wrap yourself with light as with a cloak
and spread out the heavens like a curtain. . . .

Yonder is the great and wide sea
with its living things too many to number,
    creatures both small and great.

There move the ships,
and there is that Leviathan,
which you have made for the sport of it.

All of them look to you
to give them their food in due season.

You give it to them; they gather it;
you open your hand, and they are filled with good things....

Psalm 104

THE WHALE

What could hold me,
Lord,
Except Your ocean?
My inordinate size
must obviously be
a divine joke,
but am I
perhaps
rather ridiculous,
like a blown-up blubber toy?
I am a peaceful leviathan,
on a strict diet,
a waterspout
on my nose.

My sole problem
is to choose between water and air;
but,
hunted for my mollifying oil,
I dread the whalers
who mercilessly chase me
with their iron harpoons.
I never asked
for such yards of flesh,
and where can I hide
from the lust of men?
Lord, if only some fortunate plunge
would let me come up into
Your eternal peace.
Amen.

Carmen de Gasztold
France

I am happy because you have accepted me,
dear Lord. Sometimes I do not know what
to do with all my happiness. I swim in your
grace like a whale in the ocean. The saying
goes: An ocean never dries up; but we know
that your grace also never fails. Dear Lord,
your grace is our happiness. Hallelujah!

World Council of Churches

Glory be to God for dappled things—
For skies of couple-colour as a brinded cow;
For rose-moles all in stipple upon trout that swim;
Fresh-firecoal chestnut-falls; finches' wings;
Landscape plotted and pieced—fold, fallow and plough;
And all trades, their gear and tackle and trim.
All things counter, original, spare, strange;
Whatever is fickle, freckled (who knows how?)
With swift, slow; sweet, sour; adazzle, dim;
He fathers-forth whose beauty is past change:
    Praise him.

Gerard Manley Hopkins
Wales 1844–1889

Almighty One, in the woods I am blessed.
Happy everyone in the woods. Every tree
speaks through thee. O God! What glory
in the woodland! On the heights is peace—
peace to serve Him.

Ludwig van Beethoven
Austria 1770–1827

GOD'S WORLD

O World, I cannot hold thee close enough!
    Thy winds, thy wide grey skies!
    Thy mists, that roll and rise!
Thy woods, this autumn day, that ache and sag
And all but cry with colour! That gaunt crag
To crush! To lift the lean of that black bluff!
World, World, I cannot get thee close enough!

Long have I known a glory in it all,
    But never knew I this:
    Here such a passion is
As stretcheth me apart,—Lord, I do fear
Thou'st made the world too beautiful this year;
My soul is all but out of me,—let fall
No burning leaf; prithee, let no bird call.

Edna St. Vincent Millay
U.S.A. 1892–1950

Great and Merciful God
As the trees of the forest grow straight and tall
Reaching up their branches towards the heavens
Drinking in your gifts of sunshine and rain
Help us to reach out towards you
To accept your gifts of love and mercy
To grow in grace
And to live and die in your love.

Alison O'Grady
Singapore

Lord
Isn't your creation wasteful?
Fruits never equal
the seedlings' abundance.
Springs scatter water.
The sun gives out
enormous light.
May your bounty teach me
greatness of heart.
May your magnificence
stop me being mean.
Seeing you a prodigal
and open-handed giver
let me give unstintingly
like a king's son
like God's own.

Archbishop Helder Camara
Brazil

With rejoicing mouth,
with rejoicing tongue,
by day
and tonight
you will call.
Fasting, you will sing
with the voice of the lark
and perhaps
in our happiness,
in our delight,
from some place in the world,
the creator of man,
the Lord All-powerful,
will hear you.
"Ay!" he will say to you,
and you
wherever you are
and thus forever
with no other lord but him
will live, will be.

Inca
Peru

The soul that You have given me, O God,
is a pure one. You have created and
formed it, breathed it into me, and
within me You sustain it. So long as I have
breath, therefore, I will give thanks
to You, O Lord my God. . . .

Jewish Liturgy

This soul of mine within the heart is smaller
than a grain of rice, or a barley-corn,
or a mustard-seed, or a grain of millet,
or the kernel of a grain of millet; this soul
of mine within the heart is greater than the earth,
greater than the atmosphere, greater than the sky,
greater than the worlds. . . .

Early Hindu
India

...I am created in the image of God
just like all other people in the world;
I am a person with worth and dignity.
I am a thinking person, a feeling person,
A doing person.
I am the small *I am* that stands before the big I AM...
I am hoping,
I am struggling,
I am alive,
I am Filipino,
I am a woman.

Elizabeth Tapia
Philippines

I am a man of peace, I believe in peace.
But I do not want peace at any price.
I do not want the peace that you find in stone.
I do not want the peace that you find
In the grave; but I do want that peace
Which you find embedded in the human breast,
Which is exposed to the whole world
But which is protected from all harm
By the power of the Almighty God.

Let then our first act every morning be
To make the following resolve for the day:
I shall not fear anyone on earth.
I shall fear only God.
I shall not bear ill will towards anyone.
I shall not submit to injustice from anyone.
I shall conquer untruth by Truth.
And in resisting untruth I shall endure all suffering.

Mahatma Gandhi
India 1869–1948

I see something of God each hour of the twenty-four,
    and each moment then:
In the faces of men and women I see God, and in my own
    face in the glass:

I find letters from God dropped in the street,
    and every one is sign'd by God's name;
And I leave them where they are, for I know that
    wheresoever I go,
Others will punctually come forever and ever.

Walt Whitman
U.S.A. *1819–1892*

O Mind, move in the Supreme Being,
move in the Supreme Being.

Sadasiva Brahmendra
India *17th c.*

Casting the body's Vest aside,
My Soul into the boughs does glide:
There, like a bird it sits and sings,
Then whets and combs its silver Wings,
And, till prepar'd for longer flight,
Waves in its Plumes the Various Light.

Andrew Marvell
England *1621–1678*

Blessed are they that have eyes to see.
    They shall find God everywhere.
    They shall see Him where others see stones.

Blessed are they that have understanding hearts.
    To them shall be multiplied kingdoms of delight.

Blessed are they that see visions.
    They shall rejoice in the hidden ways of God.

Blessed are the song-ful of soul,
    They carry light and joy to shadowed lives.

Blessed are they who know the power of Love.
    They dwell in God for God is Love.

John Overham
U.S.A. 1852–1941

Lovely face, majestic face, face of
beauty, face of flame, the face of the
Lord God of Israel when He sits upon
His throne of glory, robed in praise
upon His seat of splendour. His beauty
surpasses the beauty of the aged, His
splendour outshines the splendour of
newly-weds in their bridal chamber.

Hekhalot Hymn
Ancient Jewish Liturgy

Oh! I have slipped the surly bonds of earth
And danced the skies on laughter-silvered wings;
Sunward I've climbed, and joined the tumbling mirth
Of sun-split clouds—and done a hundred things
You have not dreamed of—wheeled and soared and swung
High in the sunlit silence. Hov'ring there,
I've chased the shouting wind along, and flung
My eager craft through footless halls of air.

Up, up the long, delirious, burning blue
I've topped the wind-swept heights with easy grace
Where never lark, or even eagle flew—
And, while with silent lifting mind I've trod
The high untrespassed sanctity of space,
Put out my hand and touched the face of God.

Pilot Officer John Gillespie Magee, Jr.
Royal Canadian Air Force 1942

God is the bow,
Man's spirit is the arrow.
God again is the target:

Shoot straight, this day,
That the arrow
May be one
With the target.

Sanskrit Scripture
Source Unknown

God of all power, Ruler of the Universe,
you are worthy of glory and praise.

Glory to you for ever and ever.

At your command all things came to be:
the vast expanse of interstellar space,
galaxies, suns, the planets in their courses,
and this fragile earth, our island home.

By your will they were created and have their being.

From the primal elements you brought forth
the human race, and blessed us
with memory, reason, and skill.
You made us the rulers of creation.
But we turned against you,
and betrayed your trust;
and we turned against one another.

Have mercy, Lord, for we are sinners in your sight.

Book of Common Prayer

Lord all power is yours
The power of the atom is yours
The power of the spacecraft is yours
The power of the computer is yours
The power of the jet is yours
The power of television is yours
The power of electricity is yours
Lord all power is yours
On loan it is ours
Lord let us use it aright
That it reveal your might
Lord all power is yours.

David Adam
England

Give us
A pure heart
That we may see Thee,
A humble heart that we may hear Thee,
A heart of love that we may serve Thee
A heart of faith
That we may live Thee.

Dag Hammarskjöld
Sweden 1905–1961

Great Spirit, help me never to judge
another until I have walked in his
moccasins for many moons.

Sioux Indian
North America

Have mercy on me, O Beneficent One.
I was angered for I had no shoes;
then I met a man who had no feet.

Traditional
China

Lord most giving and resourceful,
I implore you:
make it your will
that this people enjoy
the goods and riches you naturally give,
that naturally issue from you,
that are pleasing and savory,
that delight and comfort,
though lasting but briefly,
passing away as if in a dream.

Aztec
Mexico

Lord! thou art the Hindu, the Moslem, the
Turk and the Feringhi; thou art the Persian,
the Sanskritian, the Arabian.... Thou art
the peace supreme!... Thou art man, woman,
child and God!... In all shapes and everywhere,
thou art dear to me; in every form
thou art thyself!

Gobind Singh
India 1659–1708

Lord, you made the world and everything in it; you created the human race of one stock and gave us the earth for our possession.

Break down the walls
that separate us and unite us in a single body.

Lord, we have been divisive in our thinking, in our speech, in our actions; we have classified and imprisoned one another; we have fenced each other out by hatred and prejudice.

Break down the walls
that separate us and unite us in a single body.

Lord, you mean us to be a single people, ruled by peace, feasting in freedom, freed from injustice, truly human, men and women, responsible and responsive in the life we lead, the love we share, the relationships we create.

Break down the walls that
separate us and unite us in a single body.

Rev. Fred Kaan
England

O God, help us not to despise or oppose what we do not understand.

William Penn
Colonial America 1644—1718

O Great Spirit, whose voice I hear in the wind,
And whose breath gives life to all the world,
Hear me—I come before you, one of your many children.
I am small and weak; I need your strength and wisdom.

Let me walk in beauty and make my eyes ever behold
    the red and purple sunset;
Make my hands respect the things you have made,
    my ears sharp to hear your voice.
Make me wise so that I may know the things
    you have taught my people;
The lesson you have hidden in every leaf and rock.

I seek strength not to be superior to my brother,
But to be able to fight my greatest enemy—myself.
Make me ever ready to come to you with clean hands
    and straight eyes,
So when life fades as a fading sunset, my spirit may come
    to you without shame.

Dakota Indian
North America

Let us dedicate ourselves to what the Greeks
wrote so many years ago . . . to tame the savageness
of man and make gentle the life of the world.
Let us say a prayer for our country and our people.

Robert Kennedy
U.S.A. 1925–1968

Let us praise and thank God for all great and
simple joys;
For the gift of wonder and the joy of discovery;
for the everlasting freshness of experience;
For all that comes to us through sympathy and through
sorrow, and for the joy of work attempted and achieved;
For musicians, poets and craftsmen, and for all who
work in form and color to increase the beauty of life;
For the likeness of Christ in ordinary people, their
forbearance, courage and kindness, and for all humble
and obscure lives of service;
Glory be to the Father and to the Son and to the
Holy Ghost ever, world without end.

Source Unknown

These things, good Lord, that we pray for,
give us Thy grace to labour for.

Sir Thomas More
England 1478–1535

Oh, you gotta get a glory,
In the work you do,
A Hallelujah chorus
In the heart of you;
Paint or tell a story,
Sing or shovel coal,
But you gotta get a glory
Or the job lacks soul.

Traditional: Spiritual
African American

I sought my soul,
but my soul I could not see,
I sought my God,
but my God eluded me,
I sought my brother
and found all three.

Source Unknown

I saw a stranger yestreen,
I put food in the eating place,
Drink in the drinking place,
Music in the listening place,
And in the sacred name of the Triune,
He blessed myself and my house,
My cattle and my dear ones,
And the lark said in her song
Often, often, often
Goes the Christ in the stranger's guise.

Iona Community
Scotland

Should I worship Him from fear of hell,
may I be cast into it. Should I serve Him
from desire of gaining heaven, may He keep
me out; but should I worship Him from
love alone, may He reveal Himself to me,
that my whole heart may be filled
with His love and presence.

Attributed to Rabi'ah Al-'Adawiyah
Iraq 8th c.

O God that bringest all things to pass,
grant me the spirit of reverence
for noble things.

Pindar
Greece c. 518–c. 438 B.C.

Give us courage, gaiety and the quiet mind.
Spare us to our friends, soften to us our enemies.
Bless us, if it may be, in all our innocent endeavors.
If it may not, give us the strength to encounter
that which is to come, that we be brave in peril,
constant in tribulation, temperate in wrath,
and in all changes of fortune and down to the gates
of death, loyal and loving one to another.

Robert Louis Stevenson
Scotland / Samoa 1850–1894

Let us have faith that right makes might,
and in that faith let us to the end dare
to do our duty as we understand it.

Abraham Lincoln
U.S.A. 1809–1865

Lead us from death to life,
from falsehood to truth.
Lead us from despair to hope,
from fear to trust.
Lead us from hate to love,
from war to peace.
Let peace fill our hearts,
Our world, our universe.
Let us dream together,
pray together,
work together,
to build one world
of peace and justice
for all.

Christian Conference of Asia
Singapore

Circle me Lord
Keep protection near
And danger afar

Circle me Lord
Keep hope within
Keep doubt without

Circle me Lord
Keep light near
And darkness afar

Circle me Lord
Keep peace within
Keep evil out.

David Adam
England

Gonna lay down my sword and shield,
Lay down my sword and shield,
Down by the riverside,
Gonna study war no more,
I ain't gonna study war no more,
I ain't gonna study war no more.
I ain't gonna study war no more.

Gonna walk with the Prince of Peace,
Walk with the Prince of Peace,
Down by the riverside,
Gonna study war no more...

Gonna shake hands around the world,
Shake hands around the world,
Down by the riverside,
Gonna study war no more...

Traditional: Spiritual
African American

At Tara today in this fateful hour
I place all Heaven with its power,
And the sun with its brightness,
And the moon with its whiteness,
And fire with all the strength it hath,
And lightning with its rapid wrath,
And the winds with their swiftness along their path,

And the sea with its deepness,
And the rocks with their steepness,
And the earth with its starkness:
All these I place
By God's almighty help and grace
Between myself and the powers of darkness.

Attributed to St. Patrick
Ireland 389(?)–461

God is love; and love enfolds us,
All the world in one embrace:
With unfailing grasp God holds us,
every child of every race.
And when human hearts are breaking
under sorrow's iron rod,
then we find that selfsame aching
deep within the heart of God.

Timothy Rees
England 1874–1939

May I follow a life of compassion in pity for
the suffering of all living things. Teach me to live
with reverence for life everywhere, to treat life as
sacred, and respect all that breathes. O Father,
I grope amid the shadows of doubt and fear, but I
long to advance toward the light. Help me to fling
my life like a flaming firebrand into the gathering
darkness of the world.

Albert Schweitzer
Germany / North Africa 1875–1965

You, neighbor God, if in the long night
sometimes I rouse You with strong knocking,—
it's only because I seldom hear You breathe
and know: You are alone in Your great hall.
And if You need something, no one is there,
to offer to Your groping hand a drink;
I listen always. Give a little signal.
I am quite near. . . .

Rainer Maria Rilke
Germany 1875–1926
Translated by Joan Erikson (U.S.A.)

Lully, lulley! Lully, lulley!
The falcon has borne my mate away.

He bare him up, he bare him down,
He bare him into an orchard brown.

In that orchard there was a hall
That was hanged with purple and pall.

In that hall there was a bed,
It was hanged with gold so red.

And in that bed there lies a knight,
His wounds bleeding day and night.

At that bed's foot there lies a hound,
Licking the blood as it runs down.

By that bedside there kneels a may,
And she weeps both night and day.

And at that bed's head stands a stone,
Corpus Christi written thereon.

Lully, lulley! Lully, lulley!
The falcon has borne my mate away.

Source Unknown
Old English

May we, O God, keep ourselves modest,
faithful and valiant. Show us the way
and keep us in it.

> Epictetus
> *Rome, First Century* A.D.

For all that makes for ugliness in our world,
Father forgive us,
For buried grudges and carefully controlled enmities,
Father, forgive us.
For deep-rooted prejudices and petty dishonesties,
Father, forgive us.
For petulant moods and nagging tongues,
Father, forgive us.
For the repetition of hurtful stories about others
      without caring whether they are true, kind or necessary,
Father, forgive us.

> Edmund Jones
> *England*

O my soul's healer, keep me at evening
Keep me at morning, keep me at noon,
I am tired, astray and stumbling,
Shield me from sin.

> *Iona Community*
> *Scotland*

I have just hung up; why did he telephone?
I don't know.... Oh! I get it....
I talked a lot and listened very little.

Forgive me, Lord, it was a monologue and not a dialogue.
I explained my idea and did not get his;
Since I didn't listen, I learned nothing,
Since I didn't listen, I didn't help,
Since I didn't listen, we didn't communicate.

Forgive me, Lord, for we were connected,
and now we are cut off.

Michel Quoist
France

O God, teach us to know that failure is as much
a part of life as success—and whether it shall
be evil or good depends upon the way we meet it—
if we face it listlessly and daunted, angrily
or vengefully, then indeed is it evil for it
spells death. But if we let our failures stand as
guideposts and as warnings—as beacons and as
guardians—then is honest failure far better than
stolen success, and but a part of that great training
which God gives us to make us men and women.

W. E. B. Du Bois
U.S.A. / Ghana 1868–1963

When you walk that lonesome valley,
You got to walk it by yourself.
No one here may walk it with you,
You got to walk it by yourself.

When you reach the river Jordan,
You got to cross it by yourself.
No one here may cross it with you,
You got to cross it by yourself.

When you face that judgment morning,
You got to face it by yourself.
No one here to face it for you,
You got to face it by yourself.

Loud and strong your master calling,
You got to answer by yourself.
No one here to answer for you,
You got to answer by yourself.

Jordan's stream is cold and chilly,
You got to stand it by yourself.
No one here to stand it for you,
You got to stand it by yourself.

You got to stand your trial in judgment,
You got to stand it by yourself.
No one here to stand it for you,
You got to stand it by yourself.

Traditional: Spiritual
African American

He is the Way.
Follow him through the Land of Unlikeness;
you will see rare beasts and have unique adventures.

He is the Truth.
Seek him in the Kingdom of Anxiety:
you will come to a great city
that has expected your return for years.

He is the Life.
Love him in the World of the Flesh:
and at your marriage
all its occasions shall dance for joy.

W. H. Auden
England 1907–1973

All shall be well,
and all manner of thing shall be well.

Julian of Norwich
England 1342–1416(?)

I have a secret joy in Thee, my God.
For if Thou art my Father, Thou art my Mother too.
And of Thy tenderness and healing and patience
there is no end at all.

Alistair MacLean
Scotland 1922–1987

Put me not into the hands
Of any human protection,
O our Lady most holy,
But do receive the prayers
of your supplicant. . . .

For you gave birth to the One
who dried all the tears,
From the faces of all people;
The Christ was born of you. . . .

Mother of our God,
Guard me with care, within
your sheltered arms.

Greek Orthodox Liturgy

Bless to me, O God,
My soul and my body;
Bless to me, O God,
My belief and my condition;

Bless to me, O God,
My heart and my speech,
And bless to me, O God,
The handling of my hand;

Strength and busyness of morning,
Habit and temper of modesty,
Force and wisdom of thought,
And Thine own path, O God of virtues,
Till I go to sleep this night;

Thine own path, O God of virtues,
Till I go to sleep this night.

Ancient Celtic Prayer
The Hebrides

O Lord, support us all the day long, until
the shadows lengthen, and the evening comes,
and the busy world is hushed, and the fever
of life is over, and our work is done.
Then in thy mercy, grant us a safe lodging,
and a holy rest, and peace at the last.
Amen.

Book of Common Prayer

I danced in the morning
When the world was begun
And I danced in the moon
And the stars and the sun.
And I came down from heaven
And I danced on the earth—
At Bethlehem I had my birth.

> *Dance then wherever you may be*
> *I am the Lord of the dance, said he,*
> *And I'll lead you all, wherever you may be,*
> *And I'll lead you all in the dance, said he.*

I danced for the scribe
And the pharisee,
But they would not dance
And they would not follow me.
I danced for the fishermen
For James and John—
They came with me
And the dance went on.

> *Dance then wherever you may be . . .*

I danced on the Sabbath
And I cured the lame
The holy people
Said it was a shame.
They whipped and they stripped
And they hung me on high
And they left me there
On a cross to die.

> *Dance then wherever you may be . . .*

I danced on a Friday
And the sky turned black
It's hard to dance
With the devil on your back.
They buried my body
And they thought I'd gone,
But I am the dance
And I still go on.

Dance then wherever you may be . . .

They cut me down
But I leapt up high
I am the life
That will never, never die.
I'll live in you
If you live in me
"For I am the Lord of the dance,"
    said he.

Dance then wherever you may be . . .

Sidney Carter
England

Lord of the Dance   139

O God of peace, who has taught us that
in returning and rest we shall be saved,
in quietness and in confidence shall be
our strength: By the might of thy Spirit
lift us, we pray thee, to thy presence, where
we may be still and know thou art God.

Book of Common Prayer

Be comforted! You would not have searched
for me unless you had already found me.

Blaise Pascal
France 1623–1662

May the road rise to meet you,
May the wind be always at your back,
May the sun shine warm on your face,
The rain fall softly on your fields,
And until we meet again
May God hold you in the palm of his hand.

Traditional Folk Blessing
Ireland

May He Who is the Father in Heaven of the
Christians, Holy One of the Jews, Allah of
the Muhammadans, Buddha of the Buddhists,
Tao of the Chinese, Ahura Mazda of the
Zoroastrians and Brahman of the Hindus
lead us from the unreal to the Real, from
darkness to light, from disease and death
to immortality. May the All-Loving Being
manifest Himself unto us, and grant us abiding
understanding and all-consuming divine love.
Peace. Peace. Peace be unto all.

Swami Akhilananda
Bangladesh 1894–1962

For all that has been—Thanks!
For all that shall be—Yes!

Dag Hammarskjöld
Sweden 1905–1961

The Lord reigneth; the Lord hath reigned;
  the Lord shall reign forever and ever.
Blessed be His name, whose glorious kingdom is
  forever and ever.
The Lord, He is God.
Hear O Israel, the Lord our God, the Lord is One.

Jewish Liturgy

Let this be my last word,
  that I trust in thy love.

Rabindranath Tagore
India 1861–1941

ACKNOWLEDGMENTS

Every effort has been made to assign proper credits for selections. If any have been omitted where due, we will gladly include them in subsequent editions.

Poems and verses reprinted by kind permission of the following individuals, organizations, or publishers:

Abingdon Press. "Thanks for today...," page 81, taken from "Before I Sleep" from *Devotions for Young Teens* by Helen F. Couch and Sam S. Barefield. Copyright © 1965 by Abingdon Press.

Allen & Unwin. "In the name of God..., page 74, taken from *Songs From Prison*, transl. Mahatma Gandhi, adapted by J. S. Hoyland (1934).

A. P. Watt, Ltd. "Elder Father...," page 21, taken from *The Collected Poems of G. K. Chesterton*.

Ave Maria Press. "Hoping is knowing...," page 77, from *With Open Hands* by Henri J. M. Nouwen.

Elizabeth Barnett. "God's World," page 106, by Edna St. Vincent Millay. From *Collected Poems*, Harper & Row. Copyright © 1913, 1941 by Edna St. Vincent Millay.

Blandford Press, a division of Cassell, P.L.C. "Thank God for rain...," page 15, from *Infant Teachers Assembly Book* by D. M. Prescott.

Central Conference of American Rabbis. "For cities...," page 63; "Fill your children...," page 76; "The soul...," page 109; and "The Lord reigneth...," page 142, taken from *Gates of Prayer: The New Union Prayerbook*, ed. Chaim Stern, New York, 1975.

Christian Conference of Asia. "God is...," page 5; "Eternal God...," page 46; "All is silent...," page 62; "I am young...," page 73; "Great and merciful...," page 107; "I am created...," page 110; and "Lead us...," page 126, from *Your Will Be Done*, a CCA Youth Publication.

Church Pastoral Aid Society, Falcon Court, 32 Fleet St., London ECLY 1DB. "Our Father...," page 36, taken from *Prayers for Today's Church*.

Constable and Co., Ltd. "I arise today...," page 96. Reprinted by permission of Constable and Company, Ltd., Publisher.

Doubleday, Inc. "Dear Lord, you are...," page 77, taken from *Prayers From the Genesee* by Henri J. M. Nouwen.

Duckworth & Co., Ltd. "Jesus Christ...," page 40, taken from "The Birds" in *Sonnets and Verse* by Hilaire Belloc.

E. C. Schirmer Music Co., Boston, Mass. "Lord of the Dance," page 138, and "For all that makes...," page 132.

Eerdmans Publishing Co. "Lord, isn't your creation...," page 108, from *Eerdmans Book of Famous Prayers* (Wm. B. Eerdmans, 1984), ed. Veronica Zundel, copyright © 1983 by Lion Publishing.

Joan Erikson. "Your neighbor God...," page 129.

Eyre & Spottiswoode Publishers, Ltd., London. Extracts from the Authorized King James Version of the Bible, which is Crown copyright in the United Kingdom, are reproduced by permission of Eyre & Spottiswoode (Publishers) Limited, Her Majesty's Printers London.

Farrar, Straus, & Giroux. "Creator!...," page 26; "With rejoicing...," page 108; "Lord most...," page 118, taken from *In the Trail of the Wind: American Indian Poems and Ritual Orations*, ed. by John Bierhorst.

Friendship Press. "O Lord, the meal is...," page 10, taken from *I Lie on my Mat and Pray: Prayers by Young Africans*, ed. Fritz Pawelzik. "Our Pacific islands...," pages 66–67, taken from "A Psalm of the Pacific" in *Pacific People Sing Out Strong*, ed. William L. Coop.

Gill & Macmillan, Ltd., Dublin/Sheed & Ward, Kansas City. "I have just hung up...," page 133, taken from "The Telephone" from *Prayers of Life* by Michel Quoist.

Victor Gollancz, Ltd. "When I walk through thy woods...," page 60; "Even if I..." and "Thou art my father...," page 83, taken from *God of a Hundred Names* by Barbara Greene and Victor Gollancz. "For water-ices...," page 52, taken from "A Grace for Ice Cream" by Allen M. Laing in *Prayers and Graces*, Victor Gollancz Ltd., 1944.

Harp Lager, Ltd., London. "Baby's heart...," page 52, taken from "The Baby's Grace" by R. L. Gales in *The Harp Book of Graces*, Harp Lager Ltd., London, 1961.

HarperCollins Publishers. "Teach me, Father...," page 25, taken from *Poems of Edwin Markhamsel* by C. L. Wallis (1950). "To believe...," page 76, taken from *To Believe in God* (words by Joseph Pintauro, 1968).

Harvard University Press, Cambridge, Mass. "They furnish shade...," page 62. Reprinted by permission of the publishers from *Sanskrit Poetry*, transl. by D. H. Ingalls, copyright © 1965, 1968 by the President and Fellows of Harvard College.

Hodder & Stoughton, Ltd. "O you who feed...," page 12, taken from *A Book of Graces* compiled by Carolyn Martin. Copyright © 1980 by W. I. Books, Ltd.

Holy Cross Orthodox Press, Brookline, Mass. "Put me not...," page 136, taken from "The Service of the Small Paraklesis to the Most Holy Theotokos."

Hope Publishing Co., Carol Stream, IL/Stainer & Bell, Ltd., London. "Lord, you made the world...," page 120; "For all that makes...," page 132, taken from "Break Down the Walls" by Fred Kaan. Copyright © 1985 by Hope Publishing Company. From *Pocket Praise* (Stainer & Bell, Ltd., London), copyright © 1980.

Hymn Society of America, Texas Christian University, Fort Worth, Texas 76129. "Creating God...," pages 78–79, copyright © 1974 by the Hymn Society of America, Texas Christian University, Fort Worth, Texas 76129. Reprinted under license 3102.

The Jewish National Fund Publishing Company, London. "On the shores...," page 19, taken from *Alleluya! 77 Songs for Thinking People.* Adam & Charles Black, Publishers.

Lois Walfrid Johnson. "My Fingers...," page 5, taken from *Hello God! Prayers for Small Children* by Lois Walfrid Johnson. (Minneapolis: Angsburg) Copyright © Lois Walfrid Johnson.

Alfred A. Knopf/Faber & Faber, Ltd. "Each day...," page 45; "In the One...," page 84; "Give us...," page 117; "For all that...," page 141, taken from *Markings* by Dag Hammarskjold, translated by Leif Sjoberg & W. H. Auden. Translation copyright 1964 by Alfred A. Knopf, Inc. Reprinted by permission of Faber & Faber, Ltd.

Madeleine L'Engle. "Dear Lord...," page 97, taken from *Everyday Prayers* by Madeleine L'Engle. Morehouse-Barlow.

Liveright Publishing Corp./Grafton Books, a Division of the Collins Publishing Group, London. "i thank you God...," page 101, *Complete Poems 1913–1962* by E. E. Cummings.

Lutheran World Foundation. "You wake me...," page 6.

Macmillan Publishing Co., U.S./U.K. "Flowers every night...," page 19, in "The Masnawi" taken from *The Affirmation of God*, ed. David Manning White. "May He Who is the Father...," page 141, taken from "Prayer of Harmony" in *The Affirmation of God*. "God grows weary...," page 19, and "Let this be...," page 142, taken from "Stray Birds" in *Collected Poems and Plays* by Rabindranath Tagore. Reprinted with permission of Macmillan Publishing Company from *Collected Poems and Plays*. Copyright 1916 by Macmillan Publishing Company, renewed 1944 by Rabindranath Tagore. "Thou art the sky...," page 95, reprinted with permission of Macmillan Publishing Company from *Collected Poems and Plays* by Rabindranath Tagore (New York: Macmillan, 1937).

Nancy Martin. "Good Lord, help...," page 73, taken from *Prayers for Children and Young People*, compiled by Nancy Martin; Hodder & Stoughton, Ltd.

Rt. Rev. George Masuda. "O Great Spirit...," page 121, courtesy of Dakota Tribesman, Moses Mountain.

The Moray Press, Edinburgh. "I find thee...," page 85; "There is a...," page 99; "I have a...," page 136, taken from *Hebridian Altars* by Alistair MacLean.

William Morrow & Co. "O our...," page 23, and "I am...," pages 58–59, taken from *The Magic World: American Indian Songs and Poems*, selected and edited by William Brandon. "Our father...," page 55, taken from *The Sacred Path: Spells, Prayers, and Power Songs of the American Indians*, ed. by John Bierhorst.

A. R. Mowbray & Co., Ltd., Oxford. "I am here...," page 45, and "Let my thoughts ...," page 68, taken from *Junior Prayer* by Joan M. Burns. "God is love...," page 128, taken from the hymn "Praise to God," words by Timothy Rees.

New Century Publishers, Inc., Piscataway, N.J. "I am small...," page 6; "Each time...," page 12; "In my little...," page 36, and "O God, Creator...," page 46, taken from *Children's Prayers From Other Lands*, comp. by Dorothy G. Spicer. Copyright © 1955 by Dorothy G. Spicer.

Harold Ober Associates, Inc. "Morning has broken...," page 6, copyright © 1957 by Eleanor Farjeon.

Ivan Oblensky Inc. "In Tseghi...," pages 70–71, taken from "Hymn to the Thunderbird" in *The Prayers of Man*, comp. by Alfonso M. DiNola. Ivan Oblensky, Inc., New York, 1961.

Oxford University Press, London. "O God, who hast...," page 65, taken from *The Daily Service: Prayers and Hymns for Schools*, ed. Briggs, Dearmer *et al.*

Oxford University Press, Nairobi. "It is God...," page 8, and "Are you...," page 29, taken from *Prayer in the Religious Traditions of Africa* by Aylward Shorter.

Penguin Books Ltd., London. "Lovely face...," page 113, taken from first verse of "The Face of God" (page 196) *The Penguin Book of Hebrew Verse*, ed. and transl. by T. Carmi (Penguin Books, 1981), copyright © T. Carmi, 1981.

Penguin USA. "A little light...," page 19, taken from "The Firefly" in *Under the Tree* by Elizabeth Madox Roberts. Copyright © 1922 by B. W. Huebsch, Inc. Copyright 1930 by The Viking Press, Inc. Copyright renewed © 1958 by The Viking Press, Inc. and Ivor S. Roberts. "Dear God...," page 14, taken from "The Prayer of the Little Ducks," *Prayers From the Ark* by Carmen Bernos de Gasztold, illustrated by Jean Primrose, translated by Rumer Godden, Translation copyright © 1962 by Rumer Godden. Original copyright 1947, © 1955 by Editions du Cloitre. "What could hold...," page 104, taken from "The Whale" in *The Creatures Choir* by Carmen Bernos de Gasztold. Decorations by Jean Primrose, translated by Rumer Godden, Translations copyright © 1965 by Rumer Godden, English text. Original Copyright © 1960, 1965 by Editions du Cloitre. "Bad I am...," page 82; "Glory be to God...," page 105, taken from *Gerard Manley Hopkins: A Selection of His Poems and Prose*, ed. W. H. Gardner, Penguin Books.

Hilda Neihardt Petri. "Hear me...," page 69, taken from *Black Elk Speaks* by John G.

Neihardt, University of Nebraska Press and Simon & Schuster Pocket Books. Copyright © by John G. Neihardt Trust 1932, 1959, 1961.

Dr. Lindley Powers for "Sandpipers...," page 65.

Princeton University Press. "Lord thou art the Hindu...," page 119, taken from *The Sikhs*, by John Archer, copyright © 1946, renewed by Princeton University Press.

Random House, Inc./Faber & Faber Ltd. "He is on the way...," page 135, taken from "The Time Being" in *The Flight Into Egypt* by W. H. Auden. Reprinted by permission of Faber & Faber Ltd. from *Collected Poems* by W. H. Auden. Copyright 1944 and renewed 1972 by W. H. Auden. Reprinted from *W. H. Auden: Collected Poems*, by W. H. Auden, edited by Edward Mendelson, by permission of Random House, Inc.

The Religious Education Press. "Glory to thee...," page 29, taken from *With One Voice*, 1970.

Maggie Ross for "A Nun's Prayer," page 85.

Scottish Academic Press, Ltd., Edinburgh. "God before me...," page 32; "Be thy right hand..." and "Father, bless me in my body..." page 37, taken from *Carmina Gadelica* by Alexander Carmichael, Vol. 3.

Scottish Episcopal Church. "God is love...," page 48, Scottish Episcopal Liturgy.

Seabury Press. "Our Father...," page 32; "O God...," page 33; "Keep us...," page 37; "Give us...," page 51; "Holy, Holy...," page 94; "God of all...," page 116; "O Lord...," page 137; "O God of...," page 140.

SPCK. "O Lord, my day's work...," page 81, taken from *A Saint Francis Prayerbook* by Malcolm L. Playfoot. "O Lord, help me to greet...," page 94, taken from *A Manual of Eastern Orthodox Prayer*. "Lord all power...," page 117, and "Circle me Lord...," page 126, taken from *The Edge of Glory* by David Adam.

Rudolph Steiner Press, London. "From my head to my feet...," page 8.

The University of Massachusetts Press. "Lord of the...," page 82; "O God, teach...," page 133, taken from *Prayers for Dark People*, by W.E.B. Du Bois, ed. by Herbert Aptheker, copyright © 1980.

Irene Wells, "Dear God...," page 14; "What are you...," page 24; "When bad things...," page 33.

Wild Goose Publications, Iona Community, Edinburgh. "This morning...," page 6; "O God, you...," page 36; "Not because we...," page 48; "Give to us eyes...," page 53; "Bless to us...," page 68; "I saw a stranger...," page 124; "O my soul's...," page 132.

World Council of Churches, Geneva, Switzerland, "I am...," page 105.

INDEX OF FIRST LINES